Milo Learns Mindfulness

This academic workbook was created to be used as guided instruction or independent study. Educator approved for children ages 7-12.

Text and illustrations copyright
© 2021 AprilStultsBooks
aprilgutierrez.com

--

ISBN: (paperback) 978-1-7368896-2-6

Milo
Learns
Mindfulness

Academic Coloring Workbook

By April Stults

What is mindfulness?

Mindfulness is a way of being. So, to be a mindful person, you are practicing awareness of your thoughts, actions, and feelings throughout your day-to-day activities.

Being mindful is a constant practice that becomes easier and more natural the longer you focus on it. The benefits are positive effects on relationships with family and friends, ease of stress and even physically feeling better.

What does mindfulness look like?

Throughout your day, mindfulness can look like many things. Examples of living mindfully could be:

1. Purposefully taking a break from an activity because it is overwhelming you.
2. Purposefully checking in with yourself throughout the day to see how you feel.
3. Purposefully changing negative self-talk to positive affirmations. Shifting your mindset. (Negative self-talk is when you say unkind things about yourself to yourself & positive affirmations are when you say kind things about yourself to yourself.)

The point is to do these mindful practices on purpose. After a time of consistently applying these concepts you will begin to see positive outcomes all around you.

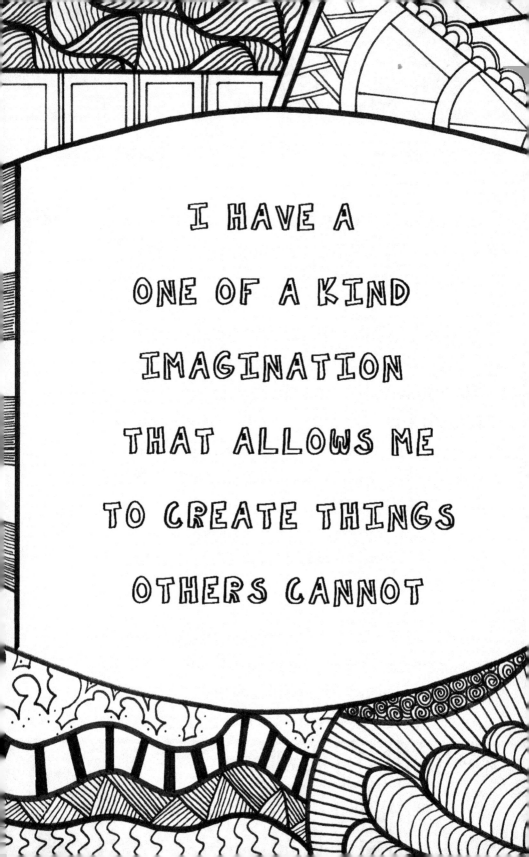

I HAVE A
ONE OF A KIND
IMAGINATION
THAT ALLOWS ME
TO CREATE THINGS
OTHERS CANNOT

```
        M T J O                   N L I U
      O B U N N X               S M G B G R
    T B A W L C C Z           G X G A I P J Z
  L V G S U P U T X G       G F B L N E L B H K
  P V S Z U M L U F D N I M A B P I H R B T
  V I H P G U E P I I X C N T F L U L U P V
  W H C E I M R E I D Y C Z N J C Y I E E T
  R D H T W N C V A J E V J X A Z O H Z E Y
  S U C O F A H B E H A V I O R S N P A G F
    E E H E Z Q S T H G U O H T P F K A M
    J C P N D V W Z N W V W D J V P N N H
      I E U B I E Z O U G X Q K F P T A
      I X C G Q S A I Q C V V P Y V P T
        M I Y A O K T N D Q I W Y P X
        V R D P V N X P Z T Y I D
          C G R J E I Q B A N W
          T U V T U U C E W
          P S T U R S X
          S A S S M
          Z P W
          V
```

WORD LIST:

ATTENTION
BALANCE
BEHAVIOR
FEELINGS
FOCUS
HAPPINESS
MINDFUL
PEACE
PURPOSE
THOUGHTS

Mr. Owl flew in to visit Milo and Lex but to his surprise, the two were in the middle of a terrible argument.

Milo was hissing and growling at Lex because he'd torn Milo's favorite toy. The yarn ball was destroyed!

Now, Milo has every reason to be upset but he didn't realize the way he'd reacted had terrified Lex.

Mr. Owl came at just the right moment. This was <u>precisely</u> the sort of situation that would help Milo learn mindfulness.

As Lex ran away from Milo's temper (and claws), Mr. Owl began to get to the bottom of what exactly had happened.

Milo and Lex always play together, this must be some sort of misunderstanding.

Milo explained that they'd been playing like normal until Lex put the ball in his mouth and shook it with extreme force.

Mr. Owl, with all his <u>wisdom</u>, listened to every detail. When Milo seemed calmer he began with a simple question.

"Milo, do you believe Lex broke your toy on purpose?"

When he didn't immediately answer, Mr. Owl continued. "Milo, accidents happen all the time but how we respond during and after them makes us mindful individuals."

"Mindful?" Milo asked.

"Yes, mindful. You are older than Lex, so your maturity matters. Let's talk about some ways we can grow from this broken toy."

"First, think about my question. Do you believe he did this on purpose?"

"No," Milo finally said.

"Good, you know that your puppy wouldn't hurt your feelings on purpose. Being mindful means practicing <u>awareness</u> on your actions, feelings, and taking <u>responsibility</u> for them."

"Lex broke my toy, Mr Owl. Am I not allowed to be upset?" Milo asked.

"You are allowed Milo, but being mindful means you go within and ask yourself why you got so upset."

"Mr. Owl, that yard ball is my favorite toy and Lex knows that!"

"Then why would you risk playing with it with your puppy?" Mr. Owl asked.

"Lex is my best friend, I was sharing."

Mr Owl nodded, "You were trying to do a good thing and it turned out bad?" Mr. Owl asked.

"I guess," Milo said.

Milo stared at Lex for a while, thinking about how he'd hissed at him and frightened him away.

"Milo, taking responsibility mindfully of our actions is easy and <u>essential</u>. When you react in a negative way, you can talk about how it made you feel."

"Do you want to say something to Lex?"

"Lex knows how mad I was at him, Mr. Owl."

"I'm sure, he ran away, but how do you feel now?"

"I'm still upset, but really more at myself for deciding to play our game with my favorite toy. Lex is, after all, still a puppy. He is constantly making messes and destroying things. It's what puppies do. I should have known better."

"Another important thing to remember is to not be too hard on yourself. Everyone makes mistakes, that's how we learn and grow. You are aware of how your reaction effected your friend, and that is very important because now you can <u>communicate</u> your responsibility of those actions. You've even identified your thoughts on the outcome of trying to make a good choice. With practice, you will stop to think before taking actions, which is the basis of being mindful."

Milo and Lex apologized to each other and brain stormed ways of fixing the torn up yarn ball.

Mr. Owl had a feeling Milo would need more <u>mentoring,</u> so he stuck around for a while.

What did Milo Learn?

Being mindful means being aware of your thoughts, feelings and actions.

Thoughts

Paying attention to our thoughts mindfully allows us to decide what is imaginary, judgments or assumptions.

Feelings

Paying attention to how we are feeling and why. This checking in process helps us shift how we are feeling when necessary, taking us from negative mindset to one of positivity.

Actions

Paying attention to how we act or react helps us take responsibility for being who we are and owning it. The good and the bad.

Recap

Milo asks Mr. Owl a really good question:

"Am I not allowed to be upset?"

Being mindfully aware of your emotions does not mean you're not allowed to be upset. It means that you pay attention to when you get upset. Reacting to negative experiences is normal. Taking time to think about the 'why' you got upset and the 'how' you reacted is essential. In Milo's case, he realizes that his reaction terrified Lex, to which he didn't mean to do. He also came to understand that he'd made a mistake from the start by deciding to play with that specific toy. It's not about being right or wrong, it's about becoming aware and not judging ourselves or others once we've learned a lesson.

Vocabulary

precisely - *adjective.* very accurate or exact.

wisdom - *noun.* knowledge that is gained by life experience.

responsible - *adjective.* used to describe the person or thing that causes something to happen.

awareness - *noun.* state of being aware. conscious knowledge a knowing.

communicate - *verb.* to give information about something to someone by speaking, writing, or movement.

mentoring - *noun.* a mentor/ someone who teaches or gives help and advice to a less experienced person.

essential - *adjective.* extremely important and necessary.

Reflection

1. Milo scared Lex at the beginning of the story with his reaction. Have you ever been that upset? Explain.

_____

_____

_____

_____

2. When someone does something on accident, how do you react? Give an example.

_____

_____

_____

_____

3. What does taking responsibility mean to you? Give an example.

_____

_____

_____

_____

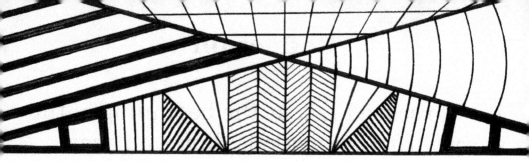

I AM
GRATEFUL
FOR EVERY
MOMENT

Dear Reader,

I wanted to take a quick moment to express how grateful I am that you are reading and interacting with this workbook.

Being grateful is another way of saying a person is thankful. It is a positive recognition that we feel. Practicing gratitude daily will help you find the positive in any situation. The more you practice this, the better you will get at seeing the good in the bad. This is called the 'silver-lining'.

I never thought of gratitude as being a mindful practice growing up but when I started teaching, we always touched this topic during Thanksgiving. You know, when your teacher would trace your hand and you would write 1 things you were thankful for on each of your fingers. These were mindful teachable moments. Later on, when I realized that I felt that gratitude more than just during that one holiday, I found that being grateful was a simple way of shifting my mindset during difficult times.

Sincerely,
April

I HAVE A KIND HEART

AND AM WORTHY OF LOVE

Journal Prompt

What are three things you look forward to most every day? Why?

_____

_____

_____

_____

_____

_____

_____

_____

_____

_____

_____

_____

_____

_____

IT IS ENOUGH TO DO MY BES

AND I ACCEPT WHO I AM

```
              Y S V D D J R K
            D O K M V P A E Z Q J E
          K J F U B L N C H A N G E P
        P Z O M V Y T M V Q H I Y R J F
      U G Z C Z J X K R B D U C V G X B D
      B E L I E V E F I U N F H J F D D J
  T N V N J N X O W H A R M O N Y U Y G B
  T R U T H Y R W Y Y B G A U N X A I L F
  G S S Z Q G M N B C U K R S A L M Q L V
  K S L X I Z R E S P E C T J D Z L O Q S
  L E B V B V F I D Q U N V H T I W W R Y
  C N E Y F L N T U Z J E T G W B N E F J
  W D D N K H F I X I Z T W X L E I V N U
  V N M U B Z J Q K V Y Q P D A D H M K F
    I B I Q L F G W P A H M G H C D P L
    K R R B I I R O O S D O M Q I N C K
      O X H K E L O M N K N P T J L H
        U C Y E O R D F K T O E Z L
          Y G J V B U C U I O P Z
            A Q X A F H N O
```

WORD LIST:

- BELIEVE
- CHANGE
- FLOW
- FORGIVE
- HARMONY
- HOPE
- JOY
- KINDNESS
- RESPECT
- TRUTH

I AM WORTHY
OF ALL GOOD THINGS
IN MY LIFE

Drawing Prompt

What is something that (bothers you) causes you stress or anxiety? What does it look like?
Draw a picture of it

What are cooling down techniques?

A cooling down technique is something we can do to calm ourselves down when we become very upset. Breathing is one of the fastest and easiest systems to use.

It has a way of calming your body down instantly but you must practice mindfulness to remember to follow the steps.

1. Inhale a deep breath **through your nose** on a count of 3-4(mentally counting)
2. Hold that breath for 3-4 counts (mentally counting)
3. Blow the breath **out of your mouth** for a 3-4 count (mentally counting)
4. Rest for a 3-4 count.
5. Repeat 3-4 times.

Ask yourself:
How did that feel?

What are imagery techniques?

Imagery is a technique involving the pictures in your minds-eye when you close your eyes. Being mindfully aware of this can help with understanding how your imagination and thoughts are connected. Often times you can use imagery to change your mindset from negative to positive or in letting go of a negative emotion. Practice example (close your eyes)

Imagine yourself standing at the shoreline of a beach or in a gentle grassy forest. Listen for the sounds in your environment. What do you hear? What do you see? What do you smell? Go for a walk in your imaginary place. Focus all your attention on this place absorbing as much as you can using your senses.

Ask yourself:
How did
that feel?

Milo was getting <u>restless</u> inside the house. Mr. Owl suggested he pay him a visit outside.

"Milo, being out in nature helps with living a mindful life. These practices are not just about understanding our feelings but also how our feelings effect our bodies. Sometimes we overlook the knots in our stomachs or aches in our arms and legs because our lives make our minds too busy."

"Being outside in nature gives you a reason to pause and breathe fresh air that is important to your well being. Air is, after all, your <u>life force</u>. Once we can stop and focus, we can understand what's going on in our bodies."

"There are also other benefits to taking a break in the fresh air. The change of scenery gives you a  chance to stop and check in with yourself. You can sit on the grass, close your eyes and ask yourself:

'how do you feel right now?'

You'd be surprised what you will come up with."

Over time, the more you practice this, the more relaxed you'll be. You'll learn the feeling of calm and ease. Often times, our feelings can be the cause for those knots in our stomachs. Sometimes, it's because we are worried but we don't stop to check in with those feelings."

"The most beneficial benefit of spending mindful time outdoors is getting all those wiggles out of our bodies. While it's true that we can have mindful play indoors, there is a freedom to careful outdoor play. Knowing when to ask for this time is taking responsibility of our needs. Imagine a jack-in-the-box, all wound up and not knowing how to properly ask for help releasing that built up energy."

"Milo, Lex is still a puppy, which means he is still very young. You may need to think about this for him. If he is acting restless or <u>fidgety</u>, he may need permission to take an outdoor break."

"Another point of being mindful is about seeing how things are without judging people or situations. So, if Lex starts 'bothering' you, stop and <u>observe</u> the moment. You may find you need a break from him or he may need a break from you."

"And this is perfectly okay and normal. There is no need to over think why something is. Judging a situation uses a part of our imagination that lacks <u>factual</u> information therefor causes a lot of misunderstanding."

"Milo, the most important knowledge I can give you is that you must be nice to yourself. You must be grateful for all the positive happy things in your life and <u>grateful</u> for the learning moments you experience."

"When you feel <u>overwhelmed</u> or <u>frustrated</u>, speak 3 kind things about yourself and then speak three things that you are grateful for. This is being mindfully positive.

It may feel weird at first but overtime the change in mindset will bring an overall sense of positivity."

What did Milo Learn?

Sometimes, being busy makes us forget that our bodies are always giving us clues to what we need.
When you stop to check in with yourself you can identify those needs and take care of them. Or ask for help.
Being out in nature can help you relax and breath much needed fresh air.
Relaxing can help understand body clues like knots in your stomach or aches in your arms and legs.
Getting time to release the wiggles out of your body helps you mindfully become aware of your needs. Your voice is a strength. Taking responsibility and practicing to speak those needs is essential for growth.

Recap

Mr. Owl explained the benefits of taking outdoor breaks when allowable.

*Breathing fresh air is vital to your body.

*Having a calm quiet moment to check in with your body helps identify needs.

*Being given a chance to release the 'wiggles' which is built up energy allows you to let go of unknown hyper-activeness.

*By practicing these skills you will learn to advocate for your needs using your own voice.

Vocabulary

restless - *adjective*. feeling nervous or bored and tending to move around a lot.

life-force - *noun*. an impulse or influence that gives something life or vitality.

scenery - *noun*. the things that can be seen where a person is at.

needlessly - *adjective*. not needed or necessary.

fidgety - *adjective*. moving a lot because or possible nervousness, boredom, etc.

observe - *verb*. to watch/listen carefully.

factual - *adjective*. based on facts.

grateful - adjective. feeling or showing thanks.

overwhelmed - *verb*. having too much to deal with.

essential/vital - *adjective*. extremely important.

hyper-activeness - *adjective*. highly or extremely active

Reflection

1. Mr. Owl talks about breath being your life-force (meaning you cannot survive without it) How do you feel after practicing the breathing technique?

_____

_____

_____

_____

2. How is playing inside different from playing outdoors?

_____

_____

_____

_____

3. Asking permission to do things takes practice. Why is it difficult to ask for things?

_____

_____

_____

_____

I HAVE A KIND HEART

AND AM WORTHY OF LOV

Journal Prompt

What do you spend the most time thinking about?

_____

_____

_____

_____

_____

_____

_____

_____

_____

_____

_____

_____

_____

_____

_____

I WILL ALWAYS STAND UP FOR WHAT I BELIEVE IN

```
                N   A
                L   L
K   C           E   K                       S   V
    L   Q       A   J               J   V
        U   C       L   C   R   C   X   M       Z   K
            F   S   A   P   B   N   V   H   Z   Q   W
                V   A   C   H   I   E   V   E   U   A
                G   Z   I   S   E   L   T   E   I   U   Q   H
                E   J   S   R   A   I   J   Y   P   W   N   I
H   G   U   U   Q   N   I   A   S   F   W   D   N   E   M   P   A   T   H   Y
P   A   X   G   V   A   T   E   K   E   N   O   B   G   J   B   V   O   I   F
                C   O   M   F   O   R   T   I   V   N   G   Z
                G   E   G   A   R   U   O   C   J   I   H   W
                N   B   X   H   X   D   Z   I   E   S
                E   A   W   E   S   O   M   E   B   Z   U
            P   R       K   J   G   D   T   F           M   O
        L   G           N   K                           Q   P
    E   P               P   Z                           E   U
                        N   G
                        F   Z
```

WORD LIST:

- ACHIEVE
- AWESOME
- BEING
- COMFORT
- COURAGE
- EMPATHY
- FEARS
- LEARN
- LIFE
- QUIET

I HAVE PEOPLE WHO LOVE AND RESPECT ME

Journal Prompt

What things do you want to learn next in life outside of school?

_____

_____

_____

_____

_____

_____

_____

_____

_____

_____

_____

_____

_____

_____

Your Thoughts

Your Feelings

YOUR DOODLES

Your Thoughts

Your Feelings

YOUR DOODLES

Your Thoughts

Your Feelings

YOUR DOODLES

YOUR DOODLES

Educator Approved for ages 7-12

Thank you for choosing
Adventures of Milo the Doodle Cat.

Collect them all!

Book 1   Book 2

For more news on Milo,
book signings, events, visit:
www.aprilgutierrez.com/Milo-the-doodle-
cat

Thank you for the: Likes, Saves, Shares,
Reviews, Story Posts, and all the Love!

CPSIA information can be obtained
at www.ICGtesting.com
Printed in the USA
LVHW010234110921
697524LV00008B/358